Short Stories

Volume One

Mitchell J. Hunt

For you, Kid

Contents

Walter & Harvey

The comments and questions of others were never a concern for Walter. He rarely encountered a reaction of any originality. Most people didn't notice at all but every once in a while there would be a reaction. Such on-lookers were usually aghast, mouths agape, sometimes with a smaller person in tow who would mimic their parent's shock before adding a point and giggle, all whilst Walter went about the most mundane daily activities.

It hadn't always been like this. Walter had grown up well within the boundaries of the status quo. He'd never experimented with alternative fashion. He'd never had a peculiar taste in music. He rarely ate spicy foods. It wasn't until his twenty-second birthday that he met Harvey.

He'd taken a walk to his favourite bookshop in town. *Paige Turner's* was a little shop on a side street at the bottom of the high road. It sat between an e-cigarette 'boutique' and a cycle shop and was so dimly lit that it never looked open. It had a basement level with classic texts and first editions. Walter had been often but never had the courage to speak to the woman behind the downstairs counter. She always seemed engrossed in a novel or busy with bookshop-related tasks so he would opt instead to be served by the stocky, bearded man who worked upstairs with the new releases and gift cards. On the one occasion she'd been the only person working in the shop, he'd managed a "yes" and a "thank you" but he wasn't even sure he'd used those responses at the right times. On this day, however, he felt different. Determined. Twenty-two, he thought, was true adulthood and so he should conduct himself like a true adult. That meant conversation. With strangers. Maybe even with attractive bookshop workers.

As he walked there, he played out the scene in his mind. He watched himself approach the downstairs counter confidently with a modest selection of classics underarm. He delighted in the imagined moment that the books were scanned and bagged. How a respectable trio in the form of

Austen, Eliot and Woolf would give way to the curious and unexpected choice of Calvino. At this, she would hesitate, turning it over in her hands before looking up at him. She would cock her head and open her mouth slightly without making any sound. He would say something casual and cool like, "hey, it's all about trying new things, right?". She'd laugh and nod approvingly. Her eyes would stay on his. She'd forget herself and become flustered when she realised she'd been holding the book aloft for so long. She'd hurriedly bag his items and tap clumsily at the till. He'd calmly tap his card to the reader and give her a little smile as he took the bag and turned to leave. He tried various casual and cool lines. Some were more cryptic than others. Some left him a little uncomfortable with himself. He settled on a noncommittal shrug and chuckle combination that he thought would be charming but still aloof enough to pique her interest. In this new interaction, he would ask her name and make small talk about the shop, making clever compliments that applied to both her and the shop. By the time he reached the bookshop, he'd played the scene so many times it felt like a memory.

Things went exactly as planned in constructing his book pile. He moved methodically along the basement shelves to gather them up. Then he moseyed around to give the impression of nonchalance before approaching the counter.

There she was. Just as he had pictured her. Her plaited hair draped over her cardigan-clad shoulders. She brought her head up with a smile and practically sang her greeting as she extended her hands to take the books. Walter reminded himself that he was twenty-two and an adult and that things were going precisely as planned. He smiled and said, "hello". They were both taken aback by Walter's confidence but it was she who showed the most surprise. Walter took this as confirmation that he had taken a huge step into his newfound adulthood and decided to stride on in the exchange.

"How are you?"

Her response was textbook. He was impressed with the quick thinking and dexterity she demonstrated in her response.

"Great, thanks, how are you?"

He felt safe knowing that she was clearly a seasoned conversationalist and, though she hadn't even taken up the first book, he decided to skip forward in his pre-determined dialogue.

"So, you must be Paige."

There was a silence.

"Paige?..."

"... Turner. Paige Turner. This is your shop, isn't it?".

More awful silence.

Then, laughing, "No, it's a pun. Like page-turners. You know, a good book?"

Humiliation hit Walter like a tennis ball to the groin. He froze. She began scanning the books. Eventually, he was able to thaw out just enough to nod his head and take the paper bag containing his carefully curated collection of classics that had gone completely unnoticed by whatever-her-name-really-was. He turned and shuffled quickly away.

On the way up the stairs, he noticed a spider crawling over a poster of the cover for Orwell's *1984*. The little creature seemed to be emerging from the eye. Walter watched it move silently over the print. Something about the spider calmed him. He leant in close to the spider. The spider was still now. Without thinking, Walter lay the back of his hand against the poster. Instantly, the spider climbed onto his fingertip and crawled to his palm. He slowly placed his other hand over on top then, as if he had stolen a rare first-edition, Walter raced from the shop, cupping the spider in his hands.

He stopped around the corner in a quiet public garden. He sat on the nearest bench and opened his hands. There he was. No bigger than a shirt button. Harvey.

Although no formal arrangement was ever made, Walter and Harvey silently agreed to be best friends. Over the weeks that followed their first meeting, they spent most waking hours in each other's company, deep in (one-sided) conversation or simply enjoying the easy quiet. In no time at all, they had learned everything there was to know about each other. Walter let Harvey in on his darkest fears and wildest desires. Buoyed by the lack of judgement and encouraged by the lack of pressure, Walter spoke with abandon about his negative self-image and his difficulties in social situations. He spoke in great detail about the loss of his parents and about how, although he hadn't been particularly young at the time, he always felt that it had cemented him in adolescence. Harvey, as ever, listened intently. Walter, for the first time, felt seen.

After a few months, the positive effect of this companionship on Walter was clear. He presented himself with much more confidence and even managed to get himself a job at the local cinema. Harvey loved to come and watch the films for free, perched on Walter's proudly uniformed shoulder, tucked just beneath the collar.

It was on a starless night in August, whilst walking home from the movie theatre, that he confided in Harvey about his wish for a girlfriend. He assumed that Harvey knew more about the girl in the bookshop than he was letting on but he appreciated the objectivity nonetheless. Walter spoke about her for the entirety of their walk home. He stopped talking about her only once his head hit the pillow and Harvey was safely in his matchbox. Harvey seemed to be deep in thought about the situation and Walter fell asleep before any response was offered.

The next day - as is usually the case when a late night conversation lapses into a deep, contented slumber - Walter woke with the feeling that a great boulder had been rolled away and he saw clearly that direct action was necessary.

Harvey seemed reluctant to accompany Walter to the bookshop but, after several pleas and promises, he relented and climbed into Walter's shirt pocket. Walter walked with solemn determination along the same route he always took but today he was noticing things he had never seen before. In the doorway of the newsagents, a graffiti artist had painted a little mouse that was shouting and holding a newspaper aloft. Walter presumed the mouse to be shouting "read all about it" and chuckled to himself as he imagined a little mouse with a New York accent declaring the headlines to passers-by. Harvey didn't share in the joke.

As they rounded the corner of the cycle shop, they were struck by a cacophony of voices emanating from the bookshop. *Paige Turner's* was celebrating ten years of book-selling. Local residents were crammed in, enjoying the free nibbles, free bubbles and, probably, their first look around the shop. Harvey sank deeper into the pocket. Walter steeled himself and entered the fray.

The party was an assault on the senses. The usual alluring scent of dusty, yellowing paper and hardwood shelving had been replaced by the sweet, bready scent of champagne and the occasional pungent waft of vol-au-vents. The dim lighting and near silence had always given the shop a feeling of monastic sanctuary but now it was harsh and loud and adrenalizing. The downstairs section of the shop was open and Walter bravely made his way through the crowd and down the small twisting staircase. Below was more subdued and people spoke in the traditional whisper. Walter could see the plaited-haired woman of his dreams at the other end of the shop. She wore light knitwear over a blouse. He watched as her soft hands worked delicately to pick out the tiny pastry crumbs of a recent hors d'oeuvre from her sweater. He was far too enraptured to avert his eyes in time when she turned. She smiled when she noticed him. Walter's face remained blank as his interior world went haywire. She made her way to him and punctured his reproachful inner monologue with a simple "Hello".

"Hello to you", were the sounds Walter managed to force out.

"I'm Hope, by the way, not Paige". She laughed and put her hand briefly on Walter's arm.

Although it would be hard to understand or believe through the prism of previous experience, the pair spent the next hour in a joyful communion of like-minds and kindred spirits. It was only when the dastardly, stocky, bearded man appeared and made some feeble excuse about 'needing a first aider to assist an urgent situation upstairs' that the conversation ceased and the two parted ways.

Walter was so happy he felt dizzy. He opened his shirt pocket to have his excitement validated by Harvey. He expected Harvey to give him that proud, knowing look and readied himself to play a pantomime of humbleness. Harvey, however, was no longer in the pocket. He was gone.

Walter's mind raced. He looked frantically about the room. He felt as though an anchor had been tied to his gut and its great weight was collapsing his insides. He moved clumsily through the crowd and disturbed them with his wild, searching eyes. He began to mutter Harvey's name as he scanned the shelves and surfaces. Reaching the staircase, he came to the place they had first met. The *1984* poster had been replaced. In its place was a poster print of a Matisse. The bright, bold colours repulsed Walter and the sounds from the party above flooded down the staircase and over him. He felt as though he might drown. He longed for the quietude that Harvey had given him. He thought perhaps that Harvey might have returned home having not enjoyed the party. He had been so wrapped up in Hope that he had neglected to see if Harvey was enjoying himself.

Heading up the stairs, he saw a commotion happening by the tills and feared that Harvey had been discovered. He couldn't see through the throng and had to slide awkwardly between the spectators and the bookshelves. When he reached the front he could see that Hope was kneeling beside an old woman who had slipped on a smoked salmon blini whilst the stocky, bearded man relayed information into the phone. Walter forced himself back past the people and out of the bookshop.

Night was falling, the air was cold now and a strong wind rolled an endless sheet of dark grey cloud overhead.. It was hard to distinguish any small objects in the unlit backroads. Walter scanned the pavement and walls as he walked carefully back along the usual route. A dream he'd had quite frequently, suddenly came to mind.

In the dream, he was young and sitting up in bed, in his childhood bedroom, hugging his knees to his chest. It was always in the dead of night and the door would slowly peel open, spilling the warm light of the hallway into the room around his mother's silhouette. The light behind her would make it impossible to distinguish her features but her scent was unmistakable - like white flowers and dried leaves, floral and familiar. She would step gently into the room and place her delicate, cool hand on the back of his head, smoothing down his coarse, dark hair. Every time, with tear-soaked eyes, he would look up to her. Every time she would step backwards toward the door and every time she would calmly say, "Of course, there aren't any monsters under the bed, dear. You are the monster." And then he would be alone.

In the dark streets, Walter felt shame and fear growing. He felt dread rising. He felt, too, an unexpected sense of freedom. His mind reached dark and dramatic conclusions and played out myriad responses which ranged from uncontrollable grief to a kind of welcome relief.

By the time he reached home, Walter felt exhausted. He didn't know what to expect and he didn't know what to feel about what he might or might not find. Cautiously, he pushed open the door and stepped into the hall.

The place seemed unchanged. Perhaps he had beaten Harvey back here. Maybe Harvey hadn't left the party after all. He resolved to get a glass of water and head back out to find him. The clouds had darkened to match the black night sky and threatened to rain. If Harvey were caught in a downpour he might never be seen again. Walter walked into the kitchen and switched on the light. The kitchen burst into harsh, fluorescent light and a skittering sound spun Walter's head. Behind him, filling the corner where the wall and ceiling met, was Harvey.

Changed now. Gigantic. A grotesque, black mass of angular limbs and opal eyes. Harvey's long, hairy legs gathered around his thick orbed abdomen, primed. Walter closed his eyes in anticipation.

Flash Fiction #1

For twelve years, there lived together

a cat and a dog who fought as such

until the cat's life was at its end

and the dog licked the cat clean

before laying quietly beside her

until she passed.

Stolen Time

Mo sat back into his tent. Everything was squared away, just as he had been trained to do. Orderly and space-saving. The rain fell lightly against the taut synthetic shell and the sound soothed him.

For a brief moment, he closed his eyes and his mind drifted back to a time in Sierra Leone. The rain had come early and the time had passed slowly before his unit saw any action.

The sound of a car horn broke his reverie. Outside, on the street, a huge, white 4x4 skidded to a halt and Mo could see the driver pushing hard on the centre of her steering wheel as the horn continued to blast. In her other hand, she held fast to a takeaway coffee cup. Mo shifted his weight forward to get a look at the offending party in front of the car. An elderly man was struggling to make it up onto the kerb with his gnarly, wooden walking stick and tartan shopping trolley. Mo sprung out of his tent to offer his assistance to the gentlemen. He reached out and gently took the man's wrist in his hand to steady him. His other hand took most of the trolley's weight as the old man stepped onto the pavement. A silent moment passed as the two men acknowledged each other. Both were grateful to be seen. Mo nodded and turned abruptly. He quickly returned to his tent and began packing his rucksack. It was time to move on.

That night, terror kept Mo from sleeping. The spot between the back of the hotel swimming pool and the multi-storey car park was secluded and safe but the humidity from the vents and the intensifying rain dragged his mind back to Sierra Leone. The metal eyelet on the tarpaulin sheet, that was draped over the railing he'd used to barricade himself in, tapped rapidly against the steel in the ceaseless wind and Mo lay rigid with fear as memories flashed before his eyes.

The first week had been easy - by elite militia standards - and the morale was high. One of the marines, affectionately known as Brick, was a talented illustrator and he drew wild reimaginings of life back home and the things they might expect to see in Sierra Leone. The far-fetched scenes of their beloved Albion made the optimistic glory of the latter drawings difficult to believe in. They'd been briefed thoroughly on what lay in wait for them and any attempts to imagine otherwise felt naively childish. A dangerous blend of anxiety and testosterone amplified every interaction within the battalion. The laughter was louder. The comments were crueler. The silences were heavier.

Mo turned on his side and switched on a slim, metal torch that lay beside him. He slid his hand into the rolled blanket in the corner of the tent and took out the wristwatch he had stolen from the old man earlier that day. The strap was soft, worn-out leather and a far lighter brown than it would have been originally. Mo didn't dwell on the age of the strap lest his approximate dating gave way to an idea of sentimentality which would in turn give way to an immutable guilt. He shifted his attention to the casing. Circular, gold and thin. The bezel was thin too and held in place a glass with an imperceptible curve. A single, delicate crown on the right side of the case turned easily as Mo moved his finger over it. The face was off-white and the small roman numerals sat proudly at their stations. Mo calmed as he watched the graceful sweep of the second hand. After a few minutes, he surrendered to sleep.

The morning sun bled through the taut skin of the tent and bathed Mo's face with a green light. The streets were quiet and it took some time for

Mo to realise where he lay. The green hue reminded him of the jungle canopy and when a recycling truck lumbered by on the road outside he feared the enemy had a fix on his location. Breath held and sweat cold, he inched his fingers towards his rifle. He found only the watch. The realisation of his present reality hit him as hard and as fast as the next memory which came too with the feel of the watch in his hand. He ricocheted violently between past and present until the two were indistinguishable.

The first wristwatch he had taken belonged to a young rebel soldier. A metal bracelet and delicate hands that swept smoothly over an almost bare clock face. He'd taken great care, when removing the dried blood, not to scratch the glass. Nobody else in the battalion had seen him take the watch. He didn't know if it should be considered a trophy, memento or vestige but he feared the judgement that might come in admitting the theft. He decided to keep it secret. In the rare and precious moments of solitude, Mo would inspect the watch with childlike curiosity. He longed to understand the inner workings and wished for the mastery to stop and start time by the tiny mechanisms.

In the darker moments of his deployment, Mo had found great calm and clarity in focusing on the watch face and allowing time to pass, controlled and deliberate, before his eyes. One evening, Brick had discovered him in a mesmeric state, sitting cross-legged and hunched over the soldier's watch. At first, Brick had assumed Mo to be asleep but, when he came close and Mo came crashing back into reality, he spotted the object of Mo's attention.

"Nice watch."

Mo raised his eyebrows, preparing a response, but he couldn't find any words.

"Not exactly regulation, is it?" Brick continued.

Mo looked to the watch again before fixing his eyes on Brick and shaking his head.

Brick shrugged his indifference and said, "We're moving out in three mikes".

Mo climbed to his feet and tucked the watch into his bergen before heaving it onto his back.

As they pressed deep into the jungle, the light of the sunset streaked between their feet and cast long, jagged shadows along the sodden-leaf-covered jungle floor before them. The battalion advanced like an arrowhead snake. Fluid and silent it glided through the flora. Brick walked ahead of Mo; two men, Taff and Rudge, at either side; and Conlon, the epitome of a warrior, led the team as the tip of the spear. Mo had the unenviable task of bringing up the rear and constantly swivelling to survey the treeline behind them for any guerilla militia that may be pursuing or hoping to encircle them. As he turned he saw the last splinter of sunlight and twisted his left wrist upward to see his black military watch ticking over to precisely seven o'clock. The synchronicity of the natural and the man-made worlds gave Mo a sense of being part of a great mechanism. He saw himself as a tiny part of an intricate machine. Integral but indeterminable in the whole. He thought about the battalion as an alien cog in the jungle's clockwork and what repercussions would be felt from interrupting the fine-tuned meter.

The answer came in the form of a popping sound and a warm mist that drifted over the left side of Mo's face and wetted the back of his neck. The next sound - the distant crack of rifle fire - came just before the thud of Rudge's body slumping to the ground.

"Contact. Contact."

The unit crouched and brought their guns up as one.

"Sniper. Three o'clock."

Like quicksilver, the team slid into position.

Dusk and death brought a surreal sharpness to the scene before him and Mo's eyes darted hungrily in search of the enemy.

Conlon's gritted whisper cut through the hard silence: "Mo, check Rudge. Stay low. Get behind that tree."

Mo slunk backwards from his position and crawled to where Rudge lay in the thick carpet of leaves. He gripped the blood-soaked straps of Rudge's backpack, hauled him across the ground and behind a fallen tree. He had known when he reached him that Rudge was dead. He was glad to see that the death would have been instant and that Rudge would have known nothing about it. The jaw had been blown apart and the bullet had passed through the spine. The precision of the shot was more chilling than the effect it had had on Rudge's face. The shooter was skilled and his position was still unknown. Mo clawed handfuls of foliage over Rudge's lifeless form and took up his rifle again. He crept back toward the remaining battalion and growled his report to Conlon.

Hours passed and moonlight now shone through the jungle canopy in shafts of ghostly light. The men were tired and the decision was made to bed in. Brick was given the first watch. Mo settled himself for sleep.

Returning to his tent beneath the blue tarpaulin at the back of the hotel swimming pool, Mo had the sudden leaden-gut feeling of dread as he saw the contents of his camp strewn across the tarmac. He had been vigilant and cautious as always before leaving early to forage behind the large, high-end supermarket and had taken no longer than no-longer-than-usual.

The sun was just cresting the horizon and the clouds took on the rose-pink hue of dawn. Man or beast could be to blame and could still be in his camp. He crouched and moved to the wall before advancing toward the tent. He spotted a pair of navy jogging bottoms laid out in the alleyway. His mind flickered more snapshots of a time past.

Their house was modest and unexceptional, sandwiched as it was between the neighbouring terraced homes. Mo had always appreciated the anonymous civilian domesticity of his home and the sight of its brown brick and dark blue front door had often been a comforting image to conjure in his time away.

The image was different now as Mo returned home in the crisp morning air with a heavy head and mouth thick with the taste of stale beer. Piled against the low brick wall at the front of the house were his clothes and possessions. He received no answer despite hammering his bruised fists against the street door. After rummaging through the black bags he found a plug and lead and headed to the local cafe to charge his phone. There was no urgency to see the inevitable backlog of missed calls and messages. Mo knew what they would say and he knew that there was nothing he could say. He watched the steam rise from his mug of tea as he contemplated his options. A heavy breath through his nose spread the steam across the table and it hung for a moment like a low mist.

At five o'clock, through the damp veil of jungle mist, Mo spotted movement in the dense pocket of twisted trees a hundred yards ahead of them. He was the only one in the battalion awake. Last watch always caught first light and the dawn had brought an urgency to their situation. Mo tried to clear his throat silently before murmuring:

"Movement. One hundred yards."

The soldiers did not stir or start but slid effortlessly from their light sleep into an alert, combat-ready position. The enemy emerged from their dark cover of trees and moved, oblivious and clumsy, toward the battalion.

The moist ground felt cold under Mo's elbows as he propped his gun. The misty air carried the pungent smell of rotting leaves and, with each squelching step of the advancing foe, he took slower, deeper breaths through his nose, drawing the death scent deep inside.

Conlon's whisper of "On my command"
thundered in his pricked ears and his finger
hungrily wrapped itself around the trigger. Each
man chose his target with the absolute conviction
of having Rudge's killer in their sight.
"Fire, fire".

The tent was nearly empty. His sleeping bag and
mat were gone and only a few containers and a
book remained. The watch was nowhere to be
seen. Mo knelt in the opening of the tent. He
stared vacantly into the corner. He silently wished
for it to be over. He wished for the relentless
march of time to come to an end. The wet
cardboard beneath the tent moulded itself around
his stiff, aching knees. Knees that had known the

front step of his terraced house as he had wept and pleaded and cursed and threatened through the letterbox. Knees that had known the cold, rotting jungle floor as he fumbled through the blood-soaked pockets of the enemy for any intelligence, information or exoneration. Knees that had known the strain of carrying a fallen comrade and slumbering infant and new bride and brick and timber and the articles of warfare. Now even his own weight seemed unbearable. Crushing and compressing him. Mo struggled to his feet. His resolve had vanished along with his possessions. He walked through the awakening city to the river and stood staring across the endless flow at the huge clock on the side of the tower.

The lumbering clock hands could not calm his raging mind. Images of his life's work played behind his eyes, somewhere in the depths of his mind. His heart raced to keep up with a picture show of the horrors and the heartaches of a human life. Cold sweat broke and his head felt light as he heaved himself up onto the stone wall made slick by the water that lapped and splashed in irregular intervals.

He stared deep into the water. The river rushed below. Swollen. Full of dark promise. The huge clock chimed. Time stood still around the flowing river and Mo stepped forward.

It took a moment before he realised that he lay on his back on the hard paving stones beside the wall. The hand that had wrenched him back still gripped his wrist. Slowly, the solemn face of an older man came into focus.

"Are you OK, son?"

Mo looked into the eyes of the man. He kept looking into them, confused, all the while as the man helped him to his feet and onto a nearby bench. Mo became aware of his bruising wrist and back as the man spoke softly and surely.

The great clock chimed again as the man returned with the two steaming styrofoam cups and would chime again before Mo had finished his own story - told at the request of the stranger.

"You'll let me cook you a meal. Yes?"

Mo eventually nodded his head and rose to his feet with the caution of a wounded animal. He walked the whole distance half a pace behind the man and stood for a long while in front of the shop that the man owned and above which he resided in a humble apartment. "*Frogham's Watches*".

Flash Fiction #2

The roots of the oak entombed the brave soldier

that, centuries ago, had fallen,

in the shade of its juvenile limbs,

protecting the very ground from which it grew

and now its great leaves simultaneously shaded his

descendant from the hot sun in the endless sky

which bore witness to all with indifference.

The Belief System

In the four years that James had been drinking here, the bar staff had never remembered his drink order and never offered a greeting of recognition or familiarity. James slunk down in his usual booth. The bubbles moved up and around the ice cubes and lime wedge in his glass as he placed it on the small, cardboard coaster. Amidst the monotonous routine, this was his moment of pleasure. A chance to think or to not think.

He enjoyed the anonymity. His outfits were deliberately assembled to be forgettable. Black brogues, cross-laced and tied with a double bow. Black, cotton socks. Dark grey trousers in a regular fit and pressed with a pleat. A dark grey, v-neck, merino wool sweater over a white dress shirt. No tie. He had been trained to blend in and disappear in crowds; to enter buildings without the key code being surveilled; to search vehicles without leaving a trace; to evade capture in high-speed vehicular pursuits. Most of his days were spent at a desk. He would sit for hours watching CCTV footage and listening to audio recordings. His colleagues were friendly but first names were all they really knew about each other. Anonymity and evasion were his work and were expected of him. Here in the bar, it was a gift. Here it worked well and James could bathe in isolation without having to be alone in his home. He scrolled through the news headlines on his phone with little interest and took small, habitual sips of his drink in a state of total distractedness until someone, unexpectedly, slid into the booth. James looked up and met the cold, blue eyes of a man in his late fifties wearing a bright red scarf under a dark, wool trenchcoat. His grey hair was short and neat and his face was closely shaved apart from a precisely trimmed moustache which sat well under a slim, straight nose.

"James Walden?"

"Yes"

"We'll stick with your working name for now", said the stranger with the slightest flash of a grin. "You MoD guys are very easy to spot, you know, in that business camouflage you insist on wearing."

James wasn't active in any field operations and certainly wasn't high-ranking enough to be a bargaining chip in any foreign negotiations. He had, once, heard of a mid-level operative being groomed by an enemy agency hoping to gain access but this man didn't seem like Russian or Middle Eastern intelligence. Not even American. James was careful not to show any concern in his expression and took a calm breath before he responded.

"Can I help you?"

"Yes"

The man slid a card across the table. It read S.B.B in large gold lettering. James picked up the card and turned it over. *Jasper Marsh - Recruitment Executive*

James looked the man in the eyes again. He looked into both eyes in turn.

"What's this?"

"It's a business card"

James gave a courteous laugh and turned the card over in his hands again.

"SBB?"

"Societal Belief Bureau. James, we've been following your work and we're very impressed. Don't worry, we've made the necessary arrangements. This is all above board. It's been approved at the top."

James stared at the card now. Something about the casualness of the stranger told him this was true.

"OK. I'm curious."

"Good. That's an important trait. It'll serve you well." said the stranger as he stood up and buttoned his coat. "We'll be in touch."

With that, he nodded, slipped through the crowd and out into the night.

The following few days passed routinely. James did nothing differently. Late in the evening on the third day, he received a text message with a time and an address.

The next morning at 6.50, James stood outside an accountancy firm's offices in the city. He faced out toward the road and carefully watched each pedestrian that approached.

"Good morning, Mr Harper."

James spun around to see the grey-haired stranger emerging from the offices. He had a warm smile and his hand was extended. James gripped it firmly.

"We can dispense with the pseudonyms now."

James smiled cautiously, "Sure. Good morning, Mr Marsh"

"Come in," said Jasper, turning back and heading into the offices.

James waited until they were inside and the door was closed to speak.

"An accountant's?"

"Why not?" Jasper said with a laugh as he strode through the office and out through a door at the back. James followed him into a small back room full of boxes and files. Through another door was a small lobby with an elevator. Jasper pressed the button. Without turning back, he said,

"This is precisely how it looks, James. The James Bond villain's lair awaits down there."

James did not laugh now.

"Don't worry, we're not the bad guys."

At the bottom, the elevator doors parted to reveal a vast, modern office space. Screens lined the walls displaying statistics and charts. Live satellite feeds from around the world showed crowded markets and terminals. A person in a state of complete focus already occupied every desk. Nobody looked to the elevator as Jasper and James emerged.

"Military?", whispered James.

Jasper looked at him, seemingly offended. He shook his head and set off walking through the bright space. James followed. He tried to take in as much of his surroundings as he could. Every desk was bare except for a wireless keyboard upon which each smartly-dressed worker typed and swiped without pause.

Jasper took a left turn and opened an office door. He stood, holding it open, and waited patiently for James to make his way in.

A large palm stood proudly in a large pot beside Jasper's desk.

"Please," said Jasper as he waved his hand toward the leather chair in front of the desk.

James sat. He noticed the artwork on the wall to his left. A vast painting of a man holding a compass in one hand and a scroll in the other.

Jasper sat heavily in his chair and cleared his throat. James straightened up and sat attentively. "Mr Harper, you've been selected to join the S.B.B as a senior analyst. Despite the title, this is quite the promotion. You will receive your salary via the Ministry of Defence as normal but you will notice the considerable raise."

James remained attentive but expressionless.

"This is a government-sanctioned division of an international organisation operating at the highest security level. You'll be familiar with many of our protocols, of course, although your training will cover it all again."

James fought to maintain composure.

Jasper inhaled and let out the breath with a sigh and a smile.

"This is the SBB. The Societal Belief Bureau. Our job is to monitor the phenomena of collective consciousness."

James' eyebrow twitched and betrayed his confusion. Jasper nodded and continued at a slower pace.

"Our organisation pre-dates even the Italian justice system and we have been involved in every major global event since modern history records began."

Jasper tapped the keyboard on his desk. The screen on the right wall lit up and displayed the morning's headlines. A plane had crashed in Tunisia and there were no reported survivors. James skimmed the article while Jasper continued.

"Despite our history, we still don't fully understand how it works. The collective consciousness. In layman's terms, thoughts can determine real world events - provided there is a large enough collective.

James drew a long breath in through his nose and turned to Jasper.

Jasper motioned to the screen and tapped his keyboard again. Graphs and charts filled the screen.

"The data shows significant shared belief amongst the passengers which spiked a short time before the crash."

James recoiled. "You're saying they manifested the crash?"

"Essentially, yes. We're able to monitor and interpret patterns of thought much like receiving radio waves. The graph here shows the spike amongst those on-board just before the event."

"But they may have been responding to a stimulus. A malfunction. A situation."

"Possible. However, the black box recording confirms that no such issues arose. The collective had an increasing level of disbelief in the plane's ability to fly."

"And so it just fell out of the sky?!"

"We don't know exactly how it works. Only that it does."

James thought. Jasper watched him.

"But if that's the case then ... then you could influence belief within communities to affect any changes you wished."

Jasper allowed a smile to grow before standing up quickly. "Follow me."

Back through the large, open office and a series of fingerprint scanner entry doors, Jasper led James into a second office space. Here the workers were informally dressed. They moved desk to desk and chatted freely. Their desks were littered with books and prints and notepads. James noticed a worker nod to Jasper and raise their eyebrow. He noticed too how Jasper responded with a small shrug.

"In 1941, the British Government ran a series of poster campaigns extolling the benefits of eating carrots. According to the posters, one's ability to see in the dark would improve by the eating of carrots."

James waited for Jasper to continue.

"You see, in 1940, the British Government had perfected their radar systems and were able to detect enemy aircraft on night raids long before they reached their targets."

James nodded.

"The Germans believed it was a result of our incessant carrot chomping." Jasper smiled broadly. "A chap from this very office came up with that one. He's retired now, of course".

James considered it a moment, "So, this is ... the propaganda team?"

"No. This is our Department of Influence."

James couldn't see a difference but held his tongue.

"Very rarely do we engage in political or military situations. Our focus is on the global community and the protection and advancement of the human race. I just happen to think the carrot story is rather charming. And you never know, perhaps those Germans inadvertently helped us see as little better in the dark as a result."

Jasper placed a hand on James' shoulder.

"Let me show you what we're working on at the moment."

In the far left corner, there was a conference room and Jasper guided James to a seat on one side of the long, wooden table. Documents and photographs were strewn across the table and, on each of the screens that lined the walls, there was a satellite image of the United Kingdom with flashing red dots that seemed to expand at various points on the map. James recognised the locations as major cities, many of which he had worked in on assignment in the past. He looked back across the table at the files and folders and up to Jasper who had taken a seat opposite.

"This is a critical moment in the Bureau's history, James. The rise of social media and the spread of misinformation is making our work more challenging but more vital than ever."

As Jasper spoke, James was able to pick out key phrases and data from the paperwork which lay between them.

"Climate change?", he murmured.

Jasper nodded, solemnly, and let out a heavy sigh. "The global population are bringing themselves ... us ... to the edge of the cliff, as it were, without realising. Most of the facts are, depressingly, true and there's much to be done but the speed at which information is being shared and the massive scale at which advertising companies work now is pushing the collective consciousness to catastrophic consequences."

James glanced at the pages to his right. Glossy magazine print showed adverts for coffee pods and electric toothbrushes that positioned themselves as the antidotes for the damning ecological facts written in bold letters at the top of the pages.

Jasper placed his elbows on the table and clasped his hands in front of him.

"We're expanding our teams here and I want you to spearhead a new division."

James sat forward in his chair and fixed his eyes firmly on Jasper.

Jasper continued, "We need to get ahead of this runaway train." He waved his hand over the papers before him.

"I'm not a scientist", said James. "I don't know anything about climate change."

"Very few people do. Yet we have a digitally connected global community of over six billion people that think ... that believe they know what's happening to their planet." Jasper pressed on, "You'll have a team of scientists for the facts.

Yours will be a truly international team. I've seen the work you did in Manchester. Your ability to understand community and individual mindset as well as your innovative approach to espionage is precisely the kind of work we need here."

James nodded slowly.

Four years in the role passed quickly.

Carefully timed media strategies had only managed to slow the global existential panic and James had begun to feel that the task was impossible as new projections and trend analysis came across his desk.

Jasper had been in the office much less in the past six months although no new recruits had come in.

In his third year, James had received a medal from the Prime Minister in a private ceremony for numerous secret intelligence agencies and their operatives. James had found a correlation between the amount of social responsibility people felt and the efficacy of their beliefs regarding climate change. The discovery had come out of some trend data from a community event in a nature reserve in Cheshire. The theory was that communal conversations amplified the effects of collective consciousness. James theorised that vocalisation increased potency. The resultant shift in tactics was risky. It was untested. But the risk paid off and some black spots for toxic air in London had been taken off the hazardous environments list. Back at the office, James made a clumsy speech about it being a team win and, with no-one outside of his work to share in the commendation, the medal had been put in a drawer of his desk.

In his fourth year, James was forced to release half of his task force as accounts were rebalanced. Again, it was unclear where funds were being diverted as the facilities remained unchanged and no new employees occupied the gradually emptying office. James had taken to drinking at work at the end of the day. It had begun as a novelty and felt a little cliche but it became a necessity and felt like an effective coping method. Now, as James sat alone at the end of another routine day, he reached into his drawer for the bottle and came across the medal box.

He passed the medal from hand to hand and allowed his mind to wander along its well-worn paths.

Did everything in existence come from an initial belief? Were some things impervious to a change in belief? Did personal belief make for a personal experience? What if a personal belief could be passed on wholesale but the benefits remained purely personal?

What if?

A hive mind for the queen bee's gain.

Weeks passed in a paranoid delusion as James wrestled with the notion and the fear that believing this idea had already sown the seeds of its existence.

One evening, at the end of a long and lonely shift, James made his way through the office. He passed each security door and arrived at the analysis office space to find it was empty. He stood for a moment, looking at each empty desk and listening for sounds beyond the space. Gently, he lay his coat over the back of a chair and placed his briefcase on the empty desk. He walked to Jasper's office and knocked tentatively on the door. He knocked again and gripped the handle. There was no answer and he let himself into the room.

Jasper's office was virtually unchanged. The palm was a little larger. The painting on the wall was the same but, after James tapped the keyboard with his knuckle, the screen on the right wall displayed graphs and data that James had never seen. A satellite image showed concentrations of huge collective consciousness events in remote destinations.

That night James had trouble sleeping.

In the forty months that he had worked for the SBB he hadn't taken a sick day. He had been ill, of course, but he found a quiet pride in perseverance and his weekends were always solitary and slow enough for adequate recovery.

As he lay there, minutes before his alarm would sound, he wrestled with the possibility of calling in sick. He needed time to think about what exactly he had seen in Jasper's office and if it meant what he feared it might.

Much of the night had been spent in feverish dreams about menacing, shadowy figures and being lost in mazes. On each occasion that he violently awoke it felt as though another puzzle piece fell into place. Funds had clearly been diverted. Jasper had been working almost exclusively abroad. The satellite images and collective consciousness radars all suggested monumental activity in remote areas of south asia.

James had saved a lot of money since he took on the job. The salary was impressive, just as Jasper had promised, but James did not alter his spending habits. His greatest expense had been his new apartment. He'd decided to keep renting after privately tracking some economic belief trends in his spare time. Even so, he did not stretch his budget and his nest egg was sizable. The alarm sounded as he made his decision. He would call in sick. He would cash in his perfect attendance record and take two weeks off. This would be enough time to fly to Bengaluru, India, and travel south through Tamil Nadu and into the city of Puducherry. This is where the highest concentration had been on the maps in Jasper's office.

The French had only transferred power seventy years ago and James knew that many intelligence agencies maintained operations in colonial districts long after giving them up. If he was correct in his assumptions he would find a SBB outpost in the city. He still could not imagine what they would be doing there.

He showered and arranged his essentials before he phoned in.

There was no answer at the office. He left a voicemail.

Over the years, he had been drawing out a fifth of his monthly wage in cash and storing it in a small safe. He hadn't known what exactly he saved it for but he had seen enough financial seizures in his first job at the Ministry of Defence to know it was a wise move. He lined the bottom of his backpack with banknotes and put his clothes on top. He checked his battery packs and packed three with full charge. He left the apartment and hailed a black cab.

In the taxi he moved funds into a separate bank account and looked at flights on an app but decided not to book until he got to the airport. At the airport he paid the taxi driver in cash and made his way to the flight desk. He knew a flight was scheduled to depart in two hours.

The ticket to Kempegowda airport in Bengaluru was inexpensive and the clerk seemed unphased when James paid in cash. The only problem he could foresee was the three hour stop in Bahrain. British government workers weren't particularly welcome and it could be hard convincing any suspicious border patrol guards that this was simply a spontaneous, solo holiday.

The first flight was smooth. James made little use of the in-flight entertainment and was too adrenalised to sleep. As he picked through his tray meal, he thought back to the first meeting in Jasper's office. A plane crash had been the first learning point. He found amusement in the irony but checked around at the passengers to gauge their level of calm. He studied a map of southern India that he had purchased at a kiosk in the airport. It seemed it would be best to travel by road but a car hire would require identity checks and credit cards. As the plane began its descent into Bahrain, James resolved to research train routes in an internet café.

The passport control gave a cursory glance and waved him through but the hand luggage caught the attention of the customs guard. She took James aside and gave him a suspicious look as she opened his bag. She carelessly tossed out his clothing, reached in and took out the stacks of banknotes. She sorted through the money and her suspicion waned. Her expression became one of wearied frustration.

"You should use card when travel," she said with a shake of her head. "Many thieves."

James had been clever in exchanging currency and had got Sri Lankan Rupee and Thai Bhat as well as the Indian Rupee he would need. He looked like any other naive western backpacker and the guard pushed the bag back to him after stuffing his belongings back in the top.

There wasn't an internet café in the airport so James bought a smartphone and a pay-as-you-go sim card from a store. He connected to the airport wifi and looked at train routes as he sat in a Costa coffee. A weekly express train ran from Bengaluru to Puducherry. James would have an hour and a half to make the train or have to wait a week. The alternatives would take roughly the same time and he spent the next hour anxiously watching the departures board for any delays on his next flight. The coffee tasted exactly the same here but James felt far from home.

Bengaluru was unlike any place that James had seen. Effervescent and overwhelming. He wished he could take his time and rest in the eye of this dizzying storm but he didn't have long to make his connection to Puducherry. He rushed through the crowds to the train station. Either he had made a mistake or the rail service had been replaced, it was unclear from the information board, but either way there was no train. A bus would be running from Bengaluru to Puducherry and would depart in thirty minutes. He had enough time to buy some essentials for the journey ahead. James was becoming increasingly aware of his skin colour. As the only white person, he stood out from the rest. He bought a baseball cap along with the bottled water and dried fruit from the shop and headed for the bus. It was easy enough to find but the bus driver was unwilling to accept such a large denomination banknote. His resistance was quickly subdued when James made him understand that any change was his to keep. At each stop along the way, the driver checked on James, offered him sweets and attempted to update him on their progress - whether James was asleep or not. He was not asleep for much of the journey. Even the beautiful landscape, through which the bus passed, couldn't keep James' mind from imagining what he might discover. When night fell, just a few hours out from Puducherry, the bus window reflected James' image back to him and the absurdity of his decision and situation was fully realised. He had been sipping his water but now a hunger was rising in him and he devoured the dried fruit and nuts that he had bought. They made little difference and he resolved to find a restaurant as soon as he arrived. From there he would be able to get his bearings and make a plan. He pulled the cap down over his face and sunk down in his seat. Crossing his arms tightly and tucking his chin, he closed his eyes and allowed sleep to come again.

The bus driver was less gracious when waking him now. At first, James assumed that as the bus had reached its end so had the driver's show of gratitude and service. The driver's urgency was in fact his greatest show of service so far. A road block had been set up outside of Puducherry and all vehicles were undergoing checks. The driver had assumed James' demeanour and his backpack of cash were the hallmarks of a fugitive and was kindly alerting him to a potential danger. By the time James understood what the driver was telling him, a soldier had boarded the bus. The tall khaki-clad figure moved slowly up the aisle toward the driver. He spoke in Tamil and the driver only responded with nods. The driver made his way passed the soldier and back to his seat at the wheel. The soldier looked at James.

"Êtes-vous français?" he said.

James thought quickly whether if it would be wise to speak French or play dumb and talk only in English.

"Sorry?"

The soldier looked at James' backpack and said: "Your passport, please".

He complied and the soldier glanced over the rest of the passengers before turning and getting off the bus. James caught the embarrassed gaze of the driver in the rear view mirror as he watched the soldier alight.

The bus was waved through and soon arrived at the terminal.

The city centre was almost empty. Across the square, two men went slowly into the warm night. It was quiet but James was wired. All rational ideas of eating and planning his next steps were forgotten. The satellite images in Jasper's office had shown the activity was close to the shoreline and James made his way to the beach. The grand, colonial architecture made the empty streets menacing. A homeless man shuffled along, stopping and stooping now and then to inspect items in the sand. James looked along the coastline for any signs of activity and could see lights on inside a large building in the marina to the south. As he made his way toward it, James focused his attention on the sounds of the sea to calm his nerves.

The beach narrowed and became mostly rock as he got closer and he could see the tops of masts and a loading crane above the corrugated iron that walled the marina. There didn't seem to be any security and James dared to go right up to the perimeter. Some old oil drums stood by the corner and chimed dull notes as small waves lapped against them. James edged along the concrete foundation to the drums and clambered on top of one. He took off his backpack and hit it behind the next drum. Sea spray made his shoes wet and he struggled to get grip as he pulled himself up the metal fence. He held on and peered over to make sure that no-one would see him and that he had a safe landing on the other side, then he hooked his arm over and swung his leg up before rolling himself over the top and sliding down into the marina.

He made his way between two shipping containers toward the building which was still the only one with lights on. A large loading door spilled light through small cracks and at the corner of the building a metal fire escape staircase led up to a door with a small window. James moved toward the staircase quickly, staying low and using the shadow of a fishing boat between him and the building. He stepped cautiously onto the metal step and crouched low, using his hands and feet to climb silently and steadily up to the door. He stayed low as he arrived to the small landing and leant his body against the door. He turned his baseball cap backwards on his head and moved his hands up the door. His fingers gripped the bottom of the small window frame. He was sweating and his breath was quick. He rose up and brought his eyes just above his fingertips.

It took a moment for his eyes to adjust and after that moment James wished they hadn't.

Inside the huge warehouse, he could see rows of people. Hundreds cramped and afraid under the supervision of brutish, armed guards. Each person had electrodes attached to their temples and they all stared forward at a screen which displayed a short piece of text written in, what James assumed to be, Tamil. The entire place would have been silent were it not for the constant loop of a voice coming from the speakers. James was transfixed. He noticed a couple of technicians moving about and attending to smaller screens displaying various graphs and data. Suddenly, a well-dressed man with a red tie entered from a room at the far corner. As the man approached the technicians, James realised it was Jasper.

He slid back down the door and his mind raced for a plan as his eyes readjusted to the dark. He knew he had to get out of the marina and he crept over the small landing to the stairs. At the bottom stood a large, black dog. James froze. The dog's snarl turned quickly to a bark and within seconds the area around the warehouse was awash with harsh, white light.

After being marched into the room at the far corner of the warehouse through a rusted outside door, James was pushed down into a chair. The door to the main warehouse swung open and Jasper walked in. He stopped when he saw James. Without taking his eyes from him, he motioned for the guards to leave them alone. The three uniformed men looked at one another before making their way into the warehouse. The last guard looked back and saw Jasper pulling a chair in front of their captive before he closed the door.

"This is ... somewhat uncomfortable."

James didn't know how he should respond but had no doubt that Jasper would lead the conversation anyway.

Jasper continued, "I'd like to believe that you're here by order of high command but that simply isn't possible."

James tried not to blink as a bead of sweat ran off his brow and over his eyelid.

"This really was a most unwise decision, James."

Jasper stood up and walked to the door. The guard, visible through the small window, stood with his back to the door.

Jasper lowered his voice. "Now is the chance to say something redemptive."

"What is that - out there?"

Jasper drew in a long, deep breath. He turned back to James.

"Out there... is the future."

He sat back down in the chair opposite James before continuing, "The future of humanity is being forged by those malleable minds. It's almost ironic that you're here to witness it. You practically had the idea yourself when you first came to the SBB."

Jasper stood again. Slower this time. Solemn, almost. He buttoned his blazer and made for the door.

"The apocalypse isn't coming, James. It's already happening. It's naive to imagine it would be a sudden annihilation. The slow, cancerous decay of our civilization began before our time. I'm determined to ensure it will continue long after."

Jasper placed his hand on the door handle before adding, "Your personal apocalypse, however, is just moments away".

As Jasper pulled the handle, James made a break for the rear exit. He threw his body at the outside door and the rusted hinges cracked and shattered. The glass panels smashed as the door and James hit the ground. The dockyard was still floodlit and the barking of dogs and an alarm siren followed his noisy escape. James ran between two containers and leapt onto the low, stone wall. He grasped the top of the metal fencing as a dog lunged for his legs. He felt the dog thud against the metal as he dragged himself up and over the top. Below him, waves slapped against the wall. He planted his feet on the fence and pushed off hard.

Two guards mounted the wall, their shouts masked the sound of a great splash. They looked up and down the length of the wall.

James took a deep breath and disappeared in the dark water.

A Love Story

The villagers tell me not to go
They fuss and they warn me
"No. Stay here", they say, "and as we are content
So you too may be."

"The rock face is sheer
And the prize you seek might not exist
Why would you risk your Life
Climbing up in search of myths?"
Etched on their face is fear
And shame
      And regret
           And envy
I turn mine away and up
To where I am bound

The climb is hard and lonely
Rocks fall and the stone crumbles in my hand
But I have faith

To fall would be better
Than to return with nothing

The sun is hot on my back and I ache
If I could turn to look I am sure the view would
be unlike any other
But I look only up

At the top I stop and try to breathe
The air is thin and cold
And in the grass ahead of me I see it
Small and delicate and beautiful beyond
imagination

It weighs very little but it takes all my strength
To allow myself to take it up in my hands

The clouds are between myself and the world
I am intoxicated and possessed by the altitude and
by this indescribable object

If I could breathe I would stay here always

But I begin my descent

The climb down is slow and frightening
To fall now and be found with the shattered
pieces would only make the villagers nod proudly
to each other
I feel my grip and my chest tightening
As I move down the rock face

Tiny falling stones from above start to scuff and
mark
And I brutally smother the object

With such force and effort upon my prize
I am incapable of moving further
And resolve to wait here on a ledge
in the hot sun with cracked hands open
Staring at this beautiful thing until I or it dies

But as the earth turns and sunlight catches
I see how the light refracts and
Expands and
Dances inside
After passing through the chips and scratches
And it is made more beautiful
If indeed that were even a possibility
And I notice for the first time its form
The shape is precisely that of my breast pocket
I place it inside and descend with confidence and
whimsy and when I reach the village they are all
waiting

I want to tell them the summit eluded me
Accept their empty commiserations
And retreat to my home and be alone with my
prize

But my prize is visible to all
It shines and glimmers and dazzles

The villagers wait patiently for my attendance at
the fire that evening

The next morning an expedition party
Sets out for the mountain

The Winner

"Tonight of all fucking nights."

The automatic doors slid apart as Toni thundered into the supermarket.

Mimi, walked in behind her, squinting at the fluorescent light and pushing her hands into the pockets of her heavy fur coat.

"It's not like I planned it."

Toni spun around. "What? Hurry up."

Mimi continued at her own pace in the direction of her mother who was already rounding the corner of an aisle. By the time she reached the aisle, Toni had picked up two boxes from the shelf and was making her way back. Toni shoved the boxes at Mimi and pushed past her toward the tills.

A checkout assistant at an empty checkout waved for Mimi to bring the items over but Toni clicked her fingers and jerked her head in the direction of the self-service tills. Mimi shook her head and glared at her mother as she placed the items on the conveyor belt. The checkout assistant smiled and said hello whilst Toni tutted and made for the exit.

A minute later the automatic doors opened and Mimi stepped into the darkness of the car park where Toni stood, pulling hard on an e-cigarette. Before Mimi could deliver the sarcastic line she'd had prepared since being handed the receipt , Toni, with a mouthful of white vapour, said: "Oh no, you're doing it now. Go use the toilets in there."

Mimi watched her mother take another long drag on the slender plastic tube. She knew there was no point arguing but she considered numerous malicious comebacks. She looked down at the two pregnancy tests in her hands and dejectedly turned back into the harsh light of the supermarket.

As she sat in the cubicle, holding the stick between her legs, she thought about how quickly the look of shame had chased away the expressions of curiosity and subsequent realisation on Toni's face at the awards ceremony dining table earlier that evening. If only she'd just accepted the glass of wine. She could have pretended to sip it. Fuck it, she could've drunk it. Why was she even behaving like this was something she intended to go through with? She should've drunk it. At least it would've taken the edge off this moment.

She thought about the terrible excuses Toni had made as she was practically dragging her out of the venue and the way she shot a look to her after each one, silently blaming.

The warm piss on her fingers brought her attention back and she hurriedly swapped the tests in the stream. When it was done she exhaled heavily and sat back against the cistern. She stared at the fur coat hanging on the back of the door before looking down at her hiked-up evening dress. She allowed herself an ironic laugh but steeled herself in case any other emotion slipped out.

The tests rested on her thigh. Two lines indicated pregnancy. One of the tests was beginning to develop a faint line.

The sex had been OK. She'd had better and she'd certainly had worse. She'd cared more before though. The coldness she felt was, in her mind, the karmic correction for such a vindictive act.

Frederik had always been kind and generous whenever Mimi visited her mother at work. The assistants were always courteous but Mimi learned young not to get attached to people that lived one typo away from banishment. The other partner in the firm lives abroad now, slightly-more-than-semi retired. Despite the company headquarters being a giant - and aggressively phallic - glass building in the centre of the business district, the top floor was mostly wood and leather and had the solemnity of an old library. It was familiar and constant. For a long time it had been, to Mimi, the closest thing to a home.

Frederik's office was spacious and accommodated every need. It was more like an upmarket studio apartment than an office and he could've lived there comfortably. Considering the amount of time he spent there, he might as well have done. It was always pristine and had an expensive, masculine scent. Mimi had always enjoyed spending time there and had often wondered what his home must be like.

Since leaving school and going to university - after a gap year spent bemoaning but, ultimately, enjoying the clichéd destinations - Mimi had visited the offices much less and it felt strange to be in such familiar surroundings whilst feeling so changed when she stood in the hall of the top floor on the afternoon of Toni's last birthday. Toni had cancelled their dinner that evening but Mimi was already at the bar of the restaurant, after travelling into town early with a carefully-wrapped gift, so, emboldened by drink and rather than feel the humiliation of returning home with it, decided to leave it on her desk. A dangerous cocktail of vengefulness and vulnerability was mixing inside her. Frederik was there.

The tests showed a solid single line but there was still time. Mimi gathered them up and placed them on the top of the toilet cistern behind her. She stood, pulled her knickers up and her skirt down. She smoothed the dress down and took her coat from the hook on the back of the door.

Toni hadn't asked who the father was. She hadn't said much at all to her after asking if she was pregnant - a question to which Mimi had only shrugged in response. After the hurried departure, the journey to the nearest 24hr supermarket was wordless and Toni had turned the radio off to amplify the silence. The award for business innovation - a preposterous golden statuette of a winged greek god - lay between them in the centre console. Mimi wasn't entirely sure where they were going or why she had allowed herself to blindly follow. There were only seventeen years between them and Mimi resented the confusing and fluid dynamic of parenthood that existed between them. She never held much hope for wise counsel in life's harder times. Mimi was much older now than Toni had been when she had had her.

She turned to see the final results on the tests. Each displayed two clear lines.

At the age of seven, Mimi had begun lying to her mother about her progress in school and the four extra-curricular clubs she was made to attend. The business was growing at a record-breaking pace and Toni was consumed by it. Mimi had only a brief window of attention and much preferred the quick praise and kiss on the head that came from reporting good progress. By the age of twelve she had a full-time nanny who facilitated any extra tutorship required to pick up the slack that had developed. Toni never had to know. At sixteen, she was old enough to read - and mostly understand - all the interviews her mother had given over the past decade. She read about a single mother who struggled to manage business development alongside helping her child do homework. She read about a woman who discovered the power of boundaries when a client meeting conflicted with her daughter's recital. She read about a woman who was determined to give her child the life she had never had and who hoped that her child would aspire to be like her one day. At eighteen, she flew to Cambodia and spent nine months travelling around southeast Asia. Her mother contacted her three weeks into the trip to ask if Mimi could remember the name of the paint colour she'd liked when they'd met for lunch the month before in Harrods.

Mimi put on her coat, put the tests in her pocket and made her way out.

Toni was in the car, with the engine already running, when Mimi came out. Mimi couldn't make out her mother's expression beyond the headlights but she knew what it would be after discovering she was to be a grandmother at forty years of age. As Mimi walked to the car she mindlessly toyed with the tests in her coat pocket and thought about her own grandmother - she wished they could have had an extra decade or two together.

Mimi got in the car and Toni twisted to face her. "Well?"

"Mum, do you ever regret having me so young?" Toni considered the question, taking a long breath in through her nose. She took up the award from the centre console between them and looked at it as she spoke.

"If I've achieved everything I have so far, despite the hindrance of having a child so early on, then imagine what I could be now if I hadn't had one yet."

Mimi put on her seat belt.

"I guess it's a good thing I'm not pregnant then."

"Thank God for that," said Toni, smiling, as she placed the award back down and put the car in drive.

Printed in Great Britain
by Amazon

22078704R00076